Debi Gliori studied illustration and design at Edinburgh College of Art and was then awarded a travel scholarship to study in Milan. She is now a full-time author and illustrator whose previous titles for Frances Lincoln include *Amazing Alphabets*, and *Little Bear and the Wish Fish*, which was nominated for the 1996 Kate Greenaway Medal.

Her hugely successful *Mr Bear to the Rescue* (Orchard) won Best Picture Book for the Federation of Children's Book Groups and was shortlisted for the 1997 Kate Greenaway Medal. *The Snowchild* was nominated for the Kate Greenaway Medal in 1995.

Debi has four children and lives in East Lothian, Scotland.

First published in Great Britain in 1994 by
Frances Lincoln Limited, 4 Torriano Mews
Torriano Avenue, London NW5 2RZ

British Library Cataloguing in Publication Data
available on request

ISBN 0-7112-0894-8 paperback

Printed in Hong Kong

5 7 9 8 6 4

The Snowchild

Debi Gliori

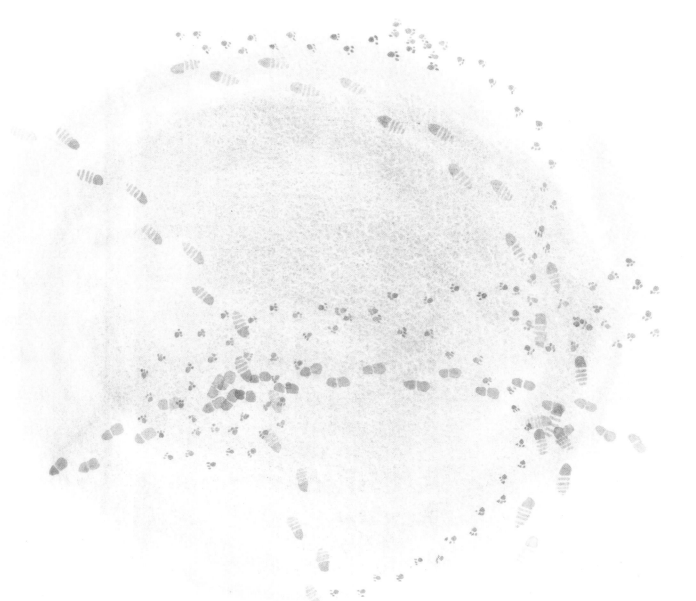

FRANCES LINCOLN

In the last of the light before night-time,
children came to play games in the park.
They played in groups, they played in pairs,
together in a circle to keep the night away.
   On the shut-out rim of one game
was a small girl called Katie. Katie left-out.
Katie-who-didn't-know-how-to-play.
She knew lots of good games, but somehow
she never played them at the right time.

In the spring, when afternoon
rain left the streets shiny bright,
Katie appeared with
a newspaper boat.

"Let's sail this in a puddle,"
she said.

The other children stared at her.

"But we're playing shipwrecks,"
said Ruth, stamping so hard
that a muddy wave sank Katie's boat.
   Everyone ran off
jumping and splashing,
trying to soak each other.

Katie walked home alone.

By summer, the streets were dusty
and tired. Everyone played
in the leafy shade by the pond
in the park.

Katie arrived with a basket and began to
fill it with pebbles.

"Let's play shipwrecks," she said.

The other children looked at her in dismay.

"But we're playing piggy-in-the-middle," said Tim.
He grabbed Katie's basket, tipping out
the pebbles, and threw it in the water.
The basket floated away across the pond.

Katie fished out her basket
and walked home alone.

Autumn came, and the trees in the park turned gold.
Everyone played there, scattering leaves as they ran.

Bennet brought his baby brother, Nick, who crawled
around in the fallen leaves, rolling his ball.
When Katie saw all the children, she picked up the ball.
"Let's play piggy-in-the-middle," she said.

Nick burst into tears.

"Give that ball back to my little brother!" yelled Bennet.

Katie dropped the ball and ran home crying. All she wanted was to join in. All she wanted was to be part of the circle.

Winter came.
It was too cold to play
outside, and no-one
invited Katie over
to their house.

She was lonelier than ever.

One morning Katie woke up early,
and at once she knew that something
had changed. Bright light was shining
into her bedroom and it was quiet
and still outside.

When Katie looked out of her window,
she saw that the city was covered with snow,
deep white snow.

Katie knew exactly what to do.
She put on her warmest clothes
and ran out to the park.

She saw Bennet
whizzing down
a slope on his sledge.

She saw Tim
wobbling downhill
on his skis.

She saw Ruth making snow angels
by the pond.
    Katie sighed a little and walked on.

She found an untouched
patch of perfect snow,
and there she started
to make a snowman.

She made a little snowball,
then she patted on more snow
until it was big enough to roll on
the ground, round and round,
till the snowball
came up to
her tummy.
That was the
snowman's body.

Then Katie made a smaller
ball for the snowman's head.
She carefully lifted the head
on to the body and stood back
to admire it.

The snowman was very
small, not really as big
as a man at all.

"I know what you are," said Katie.
"You're a Snowchild! But poor you,
you haven't any eyes
or even a smile, and
you must be frozen
without a hat. Wait there,
and I'll run home and find
some things for you."

Katie rushed home and started to fill a basket
for her Snowchild. He'll need these, she thought,
picking up some things in the garden shed.

And this will be good, she thought, taking
something from the kitchen.

She found something else under Mum
and Dad's bed and the very last thing
on the chair in her bedroom.
Then she rushed outside again.

She ran and ran, past Bennet, past Tim, past Ruth -
and then she stopped in surprise.

There, beside her Snowchild, was another snowman.
It didn't have any eyes or smile either.

"Poor thing," said Katie.
"Once I've finished
my Snowchild, I'll run
home for some
bits for you."
   She put her basket down
and unpacked it.
First, two bits of coal for
the eyes and a carrot for the nose.
Then Katie drew a smile with her finger.

Last of all, she put
a woolly hat on the
Snowchild's head and
tenderly wrapped
a scarf around
where its head
joined its body.
She patted the
Snowchild and
he seemed to
smile back.

"What a brilliant snowman," said a voice.

Katie looked round, and from behind the unfinished snowman
stepped a small girl carrying a bag.

   "Look, I've brought some wool to make hair for mine,"
she said. "I'm going to call her Jenny, like me.
What's yours called?"

   "I'm calling him Snowchild
because he's so small," said Katie.

"When I finish this one," said Jenny, "let's make a really huge snowman together."

Katie's smile grew wider than her Snowchild's.

"A Snowdad," she laughed.

"And a Snowmum," hooted Jenny.

"With some Snowfriends," said Katie.

"Just like us," said Jenny.

By the time darkness fell,
the park was full of friends:
snowfriends, snowchildren,
real friends and real
children who played
and laughed and
rolled in the snow.

And Katie wasn't watching them
from the shut-out rim.
She was there in the circle,
playing with her new friend.

MORE PICTURE BOOKS IN PAPERBACK
FROM FRANCES LINCOLN

LITTLE BEAR AND THE WISH FISH
Debi Gliori

The bears of Papana River Valley lead a charmed life, but that doesn't
stop them complaining. So the Raindancer, the Sunblazer and the Snowmaker
send a Wish Fish to teach them a lesson they will never forget!

Suitable for National Curriculum English - Reading Key Stage 1
Scottish Guidelines English Language - Reading, Levels A and B

ISBN 0-7112-0986-3

THE FIRE CHILDREN
Eric Maddern

Frané Lessac

Why are some people black, some white, and others yellow, pink or brown?
This intriguing West African creation myth tells how the first spirit-people
solve their loneliness using clay and fire - and fill the Earth with children
of every colour under the sun!
Selected for Children's Books of the Year 1993

Suitable for National Curriculum English - Key Stages 1 and 2;
Scottish Guidelines English Language - Reading, Levels B and C;
Environmental Studies - Level C

ISBN 0-7112-0885-9

ANANCY AND MR DRY-BONE
Fiona French

Penniless Anancy and rich Mr Dry-Bone both want to marry Miss Louise, but *she*
wants to marry the man who can make her laugh. An original story, based on
characters from traditional Caribbean and West African folk tales.

Selected for Children's Books of the Year 1992
Shortlisted for the Kate Greenaway Award 1992
Winner of the Sheffield Book Award 1992, Category 0 - 6 years

Chosen as part of the recommended booklist for the National Curriculum Key Stage 2,
English Task 1997: Reading, Levels 1-2
Suitable for National Curriculum English - Reading, Key Stages 1 and 2
Scottish Guidelines English Language - Reading, Levels A and B

ISBN 0-7112-0787-9

Frances Lincoln titles are available from all good bookshops.